# PARKER GROWS A GARDEN

by **Parker Curry & Jessica Curry**
illustrated by **Brittany Jackson & Tajaé Keith**

Ready-to-Read

Simon Spotlight
New York London Toronto Sydney New Delhi

I dedicate this book to my Mommy.
—P. C.

Dedicated to my sweet children:
if I had a flower for each time they made me smile,
I could walk in my garden until the end of time.
—J. C.

SIMON SPOTLIGHT
An imprint of Simon & Schuster Children's Publishing Division
1230 Avenue of the Americas, New York, New York 10020
This Simon Spotlight edition December 2022

Manufactured in the United States of America 1022 LAK
2 4 6 8 10 9 7 5 3 1
Library of Congress Cataloging-in-Publication Data
Names: Curry, Parker, author. | Curry, Jessica, author. | Jackson, Bea, 1986– illustrator. | Keith, Tajaé, illustrator. Title: Parker grows a garden / by Parker Curry & Jessica Curry ; illustrated by Brittany Jackson, Tajaé Keith. Description: New York : Simon Spotlight, 2022. | Series: A Parker Curry book | Summary: "Parker grows a backyard garden with her two grandmothers, Nana and Mom Mom"—Provided by publisher. Identifiers: LCCN 2022015070 (print) | LCCN 2022015071 (ebook) | ISBN 9781665931021 (paperback) | ISBN 9781665931038 (hardcover) | ISBN 9781665931045 (ebook) Subjects: CYAC: Curry, Parker—Childhood and youth—Fiction. | African Americans—Fiction. | Gardens—Fiction. | Grandmothers—Fiction. | LCGFT: Picture books. Classification: LCC PZ7.1.C8665 Pap 2022 (print) | LCC PZ7.1.C8665 (ebook) | DDC [E]—dc23
LC record available at https://lccn.loc.gov/2022015070
LC ebook record available at https://lccn.loc.gov/2022015071

My name is Parker.
I am visiting
my Nana today.

Nana loves growing flowers in her garden.

Now I am almost
as tall as her rosebush.

I wish I could have
my own garden too.

“Wonderful idea!”
my mom says.

I find a sunny spot
in my backyard.

My family helps
prepare the soil.

In the fall Nana brings
a tray of tulip bulbs.

We dig holes
and plant them
in the soil.

“Bulbs need water
to grow roots,”
says Nana.

She gives me
a shiny watering can.

Nana says my garden will bloom in the spring.

I wait and wait and wait.

While I wait,
I draw pictures
of my tulip garden.

Pink tulips
are my favorite!

When the snow melts,
Mom Mom visits.

She helps me plant
cucumbers and herbs.

"Look! A worm!"
I shout.

"Worms are important
for healthy soil,"
my grandma explains.

One sunny day
I finally see green shoots
and leafy vines
poking out of the ground!

Soon my garden blooms!
I spy hummingbirds.

I smell the herbs . . .

but not before

I check for bees!

We invite my grandmas
for a special dinner.

“These cucumbers are so crunchy!” says Nana.

“And the tulips are
as pretty as Parker!”
adds Mom Mom.

I love my grandmas!

And I love my garden!

# GOING ON A NATURE WALK

Parker loves taking nature walks to see what is blooming in her neighborhood.

In the spring Parker looks forward to the cherry blossom trees. When the wind blows, cherry blossom petals rain down on her head!

In the summer Parker sees many different colors of hydrangea flowers. In the fall she sees squirrels gathering acorns. In the winter she looks for holly trees.

Nature walks are a fun way to spend time with family and friends. Wherever you live, there is always something new to discover outside!